HYPE

and other writings

by various authors

edited by James Doyle

Hype and Other Writings: 1st Edition
Published 09/04/2011

Published by Lulu Publishing
Copyright © 2011
James Doyle

ISBN 978-1-105-33329-3

Printed in US by Lulu Publishing

Lulu.com

TABLE OF CONTENTS

Hype

by Jaishreeramanujanchandaranjanbalasubramaniam Dasunavaninkumpuf

Hype
by Jaishreeramanujanchandaranjanbalasubramaniam Dasunavaninkumpuf

(Kala opens door and peeks into the room. He looks around, sees no one, breathes a sigh of relief, and enters. He goes over to the wall, picks up an apron and puts it on. He goes to the espresso machine, makes two shots of espresso, froths milk, pumps flavor shots, pours it all into a cup and puts on a lid while looking around nervously. He smells the drink, smiles, and takes a sip)

Ms. D: HEY!

Kala: *(Spits out coffee)*

Ms. D: You're late.

Kala: I know Ms. Dour. Sorry.

Ms. D: Sorry you're late or sorry for the mess?

Kala: Uh. Both?

Ms. D: Good. But be MORE sorry about being late. The mess you can fix...

Kala: I know. I will. And sorry I'm late. It's just...

Ms. D: I don't need excuses Kala. I need you to be on time. "At Espresso Express –

Kala: - We have a zero tolerance policy on tardy train conductors" I know.

Ms. D: Our customers depend on us to caffeinate their mornings.

Kala: I was up late studying for a test and I must've slept through the alarm.

Ms. D: Look Kala. I like you but you need to be on time every time or...

Kala: No. Please. I need this job to pay for school. I'll be on time. I promise.

Gina: Hi Kala... *(winks)*

Kala: Ah! Gina! Were you here the whole time?

Gina: Yep. *(blows him a kiss)*

Kala: Wow. I did NOT notice you.

Gina: *(sad)* Oh. It's ok. It's good. Skgood.

Kala: Well don't just stand there... put on your apron. The doors open in 5... 4... 3... 2... 1...

INTRO

Kala: Good morning! Welcome to Espresso Express. *(reluctantly)* Chuga chuga woot... woot... what can I make for you today?

Customer 1: *(tweaking out)* I'll *(twitch)* just *(twitch)* have *(twitch)* the usual...

Kala: Okay, Tom. And remember, you enter through the door, we close at 9, just because you can see through the window doesn't mean you can come in, and after we lock the doors, we mean it.

Customer 1: T...t...t...totally. *(twitch)* I get it. *(twitch)* Better give me two then.

Kala: Two large cups filled to the top with espresso shots. Coming right up.

Customer 1: Th... th... th... thanks Kala. *(twitch)* Nyaaah! *(twitch twitch twitch)*

Kala: No problem Tom...

Ms. D: I can see today is going to be another disaster. I'm surrounded by morons.

Gina: Like the guys with all the wives?

Kala: Morons not Mormons moron.

Gina: Oh... I don't' get it.

Ms. D: We know. Kala, I'll be back in a couple hours. Try to hold this place together... Don't screw this up!

Kala: No! Please don't go! You can't leave me with –

Gina: So Kala *(flips her hair, adjusts her self, tries to look cute)* Wassup?

Kala: The sky...

Gina: Unhahahahaha. Good one. Hey Kala... do you know what today is?

Kala: Uh. Tuesday.

Gina: Nope. It's our anniversary!

Kala: What?!

Gina: Today is the 100th day I've know you!

Kala: Wow. It feels like so much longer. And that's not how anniversaries work...

Gina: So to celebrate I've got a question for you...

Kala: Uh. Here we go again. Alright... let's get this over with.

Gina: I was wondering if this Saturday... you and I could –

Kala: I'm busy this Saturday. I'm meeting with a tutor to keep my grades up.

Gina: I thought you had all "A" s.

Kala: I do.

Gina: Oh... Well maybe Friday?

Kala: Gina, look, I don't have time for a social life and if I did it wouldn't be with you.

Gina: Oh... Ok... No worries... It's good. Skgood.

Kala: Can we just focus on work Gina. Please. I can't lose this job.

Gina: Sure. Yeah. Sure. No problem. Hi. Welcome to Espresso Express.

Mom: Where is my boy?

Kala: Mom? What are you doing here?

Mom: Your report card came today.

Kala: Oh. All "A" s again?

Mom: Kala... I don't know how to say this... you got... a "B"

Kala: What?!

Mom: Do you want to work in a coffee shop the rest of your life?

Kala: No.

Mom: Your father and I told you that you would go into Medicine, or Engineering… but with grades like this… You're going to end up going into *(sobs)* accounting… or… *(with dread)* business…

Kala: What's wrong with going into business?

Mom: *(reacts)* I did not bring you into this world to make any less than 6 figures!

Kala: But Mom, what if I don't want to do ANY of those things?

Mom: Do I look like a vampire?

Kala: No…

Mom: Then why are you driving a stake through my heart?!

Kala: Mom… listen. What if I wanted to study… something else? Like… music…?

Mom: *(reacts)* Do not tell that joke to your father. Do you want to aggravate his drinking problem?

Kala: Mom, Dad doesn't drink…

Mom: Not yet! But that's only because I told him your "B" was an infinity symbol.

Kala: Mom. There is nothing wrong with a –

Mom: *(Shushing him)* Bup bup bup bup bup. Just fix this Kala. *(leaving)* Study harder. Bribe your teachers. Do you have Aspergers?! Here, take some Ritalin! I don't care how you do it. Just fix it!

Kala: *(sighs)* Ok… I'm on it… Bye Mom…

Gina: What was that about?

Kala: I got a "B" in one of my classes…

Gina: Nice.

Kala: No Gina. No. Not nice. A "B" is an Indian "F"…

Gina: I guess an "F" is a Gina "B" then!

Kala: Never mind. You wouldn't understand. Just help the next customer…

Gina: Hello welcome to Espresso Express! Chuga chuga woot woot! What can I get for you?

Customer 2: I'll have one medium latte. Fat free.

Gina: Why do you think you're fat?

Customer 2: What?

Gina: Just kidding. HA!

Kala: Gina. Woah. What the –

Gina: Forget I said it! *(to customer)* Sorry. Stud muffin's gettin' teste.

Kala: Gina! Stop!

Gina: Which reminds me can I get you a delicious ChocaWaka LocoMuffin?

Customer 2: No... thanks... just a latte. I'm late.

Gina: It' pronounced latte.

Customer 2: Yes. Yes. Just that.

Gina: Just what? A latte or a late because we don't serve the latter.

Customer 2: No LocoMuffin. No latter. No late. Just a latte.

Gina: Are you sure? They're dark and delicious like lover-boy over here...

Kala: GAH! Why do you like me? We have nothing in common!

Gina: I dunno. You're dangerous... like a gangster. Or a terrorist.

Kala: Excuse me?

Gina: You know like someone from Kazakystan or whatever...

Kala: Gina... I told you... I'm Indian.

Gina: Yeah. Not white. Indian. Whatever.

Kala: No, Gina. Not whatever. I'm Indian.

Gina: If you're an Indian then what's your tribal name?

Kala: *(reacts)* Gina. I'm this kind of Indian not this kind of Indian.

Gina: Uh...

Kala: *(sighs)* Fine. It's Chief Fuzzywuzzywasabear.

Gina: NUH-UH! *(beat)* prove it.

Kala: *(unbuttons shirt)* See? I have no hair.

Gina: Oh, so clean! He really wasn't fuzzy was he?

Customer 2: I don't care! *(beat)* I just want a latte!

Kala: You're a little slow aren't you Gina?

Gina: No way Jose. I run a 6 minute mile.

Kala: Okay. I need to end this conversation before it gets embarrassing.

Gina: Don't worry about it. I mean you're a little awkward but you're doing fine...

Customer 2: Can I PLEASE get –

Kala: One latte. On the house. Sorry for the wait.

Gina: Hello. Welcome to Espresso Express! What can I get for you?

Rob: One steaming hot cup of Kala.

Gina: Ooo. Sounds delicious.

Rob: Aye Kala!

Kala: Oh. Hey Rob.

Rob: Hey man! What's up?

Kala: Oh not much. Life's kickin' my –

Rob: Awesome. So listen man. Killer party on Saturday! You got to be there!

Kala: Ah. I wish I could Rob but I need to meet with my tutor on Saturday.

Rob: Oh come on man! It won't be the same with out you! You have to!

Kala: Uh…

Rob: Just be there! Ok? See you Saturday! Don't let us down! *(leaves)*
Kala: Ah! When are people going to understand that I am a busy person!

Customer 3: Uh… Excuse me…

Kala: I have responsibilities! I have goals! Maybe not MY goals… But I have them!

Customer 3: Excuse me…

Kala: I just…

Customer 3: Excuse ME!

Kala: WHAT?!

Customer 3: Every time I drink my coffee I get a stabbing pain in my right eye.

Kala: Really?! YOU MIGHT HAVE DIABETEIS.

Customer 3: REALLY?!?!

Kala: No. Just take out the spoon out.

Customer 3: Oh…

Gina: Kala… are you doing ok? You're acting kind of…

Kala: Back off Gina! I will flip… No. Not like a gymnast. *(phone rings)* Hello?

Ms. D: *(on phone)* Kala! I have big news! The CEO of Espresso Express is coming to visit OUR store today!

Kala: What? Woah!

Ms. D: I Know. He's going to be there in 5 minutes. And he has an order…

Kala: Uh-huh… Uh-huh… Uh-huh… Oh, and is that it? Okay. Have a good day. Okay, buh-bye. Gina. Gina? Gina?! This is the mother-load! This is code red! Call code blue! Code green! Call the whole damn rainbow if you have to!

Gina: What? What happened?!

Kala: Get everything ready! Make 10 of everything! CEO! AHH!

Gina: Why are you screaming?! Stop screaming at me! My ears! Ow! I think I'm bleeding!

Kala: Ugh! Never mind! I'll do this myself, just like everything else!
(Kala starts making drinks)

Ms. D: Stop being late! And don't screw anything up!
(making drinks, slightly freaking out)

Mom: Your grades are too low! You're a failure! Ritalin!
(making drink, more freaking out)

Rob: Come on, this party is about to be crackin'! Don't let us down!
(finishing drinks, really freaking out)

Kala: Finally!

Ms. D: We're here! I hope everything is –

Kala: Yep! It's right here we g— *(spills drinks all over her)*

Ms. D: Kala! You've ruined it! You're a failure! Get out of my sight before you ruin something else!

Kala: *(Sobbing crazily)*

Gina: Kala, chill out dude.

Kala: No YOU chill out dude! I'm freakin' out here man!

Gina: I'm a girl.

Kala: Jesus Christ in America! I've never met anyone so... so... DUMB!

Gina: Oh... I see... I'm... I'm dumb... So it's me. I'm the problem.

Kala: What? No. No. Gina, I'm sorry. It's not you...I'm mean it's a little bit you. But it's my boss. My teachers. My parents. My friends. Everybody's expecting so much of me. I'm just afraid I won't live up to the hype.

Gina: So I'm not dumb?

Kala: Uh... Yeah. Sure. Why not.

Gina: Look Kala… maybe you're expecting too much of yourself. You're only human.

Kala: I appreciate the thought but you don't know what it's like

Gina: To constantly fall short of people's expectations?

Kala: Yeah. You never worry about what other people think. Or anything, really…

Gina: Actually. I do. I mean look at me Kala… I know I'm not the best and the brightest. I'm always disappointing people. Even myself. But I believe that in today's society, everyone experiences a lapse in self confidence mostly stemming from the psychological fact that our sub-conscious is constrained by our own conscious when in reality, everyone has something to offer.

Kala: Woah, where'd that come from?

Gina: …What? Look, Kala. So maybe I'm going to work here the rest of my life… but what's wrong with that? People need coffee don't they?

Kala: I guess so…

Gina: So I'll be here to make it for them. And maybe put a smile on their face. So what if you're a failure and you can't do anything right and you screw things up and you're going to lose all your friends and life pretty much hates you

Kala: I get it!

Gina: …I think all that makes you worth something… don't you? *(looks at clock)* Well… that's the end of my shift. I'll see you tomorrow Kala. *(starts to leave)*

Kala: Hey Gina?

Gina: Yeah?

Kala: How about that date… This Saturday? There's this party we should go to…

Gina: But… I thought you needed to meet with your tutor…

Kala: Yeah, well… I think I can learn more from someone else. *(smiles)*

Gina: Oh yeah? Who? *(Pause, Realizes)* Oh…

Kala: *(smiles)* I'll see you tomorrow Gina.

Gina: Ok. Awesome sounds good see you tomorrow sounds good it's good Skgood.

Kala: *(watches her leave, picks up phone, dials)* Hello? Hi Mom. I need to tell you something... But first, can you do something for me? Great. Pour Dad a drink. And keep that Ritalin comin'!

As God Walked from Door to Window

By Sam Munson

As God Walked from Door to Window   by Sam Munson

(Reaches up and pulls a cord to turn on the light, looks around and slowly turns to profile, still looking. Sees something) Ah! Here we go. *(Pulls a box off a shelf and begins to sort through the objects inside.)* All pretty standard. A few stuffed animals, some board games... Battleship, a classic... and, ah! Of course... Teenage Mutant Ninja Turtle action figures... *(playing with it)* Yaw... I wanted to be Michelangelo in the worst way...You know, I actually grew up in the apartments around the corner... the apartments above the pizza place? Eddie's... Great sauce. Well, I kind of grew up there. When I was little I was always in daycare. And that's where I met Thomas.

INTRO

When I met Thomas, he looked... ridiculous. He was skinny and pale and quiet and nobody really talked to him. That is until one day we got partnered up for board games. And my partner? Was Thomas. Great. The weird kid. That's what I thought. So anyways, Thomas and I sit down at the first board game... Battleship... and he beats me. Badly. It was terrible. Well, Thomas could see this bothered me... and so the next game – he lets me win. He does. Moves his ships around to wherever I guess. Now I can't prove that's what happened. And he would never tell me if he did... it was always,

Thomas: "I don't know what you're talkin' about. You won that game fair and square."

But I'm pretty sure that's what went down. And that was actually the moment I fell for him. Right there, at 11 years old over a game of Battleship. But... About 5 years later *he* was actually the one that kissed *me*. We were just sitting there watching T.V. after school like normal and he kissed me. Out of the blue.

There's this guy named Aristotle, maybe you've heard of him. He said, "Love is composed of a single soul inhabiting two bodies." Beautiful isn't it? But it's right, it's absolutely spot on. We were just connected.

But, uh... nobody's perfect. Ya, know? I always knew Thomas was... that something wasn't quite right. But it took a few years for him to tell me about his depression and anxiety and... well, everything else. But, I shouldn't have been surprised. He was always going through mood swings, sometimes crazy, fast, violent, scary mood swings. More because of the medications then what was going on his head... I think. And, I was there for him and the late night phone calls, and the periods of seclusion, even the suicide attempts and the times he looked at me and told me to go to hell because "he didn't love me or anybody else and I should just disappear."

When my Mom died he wasn't at the funeral. He, he just couldn't get out of bed. I was crying for... oh, God... days. After a few days he did finally work up the energy to say something about it. He, uh, just tried to fix it the only way he knew how.

Thomas: "Here, take a couple of these. It'll make you feel better."

How can I blame him for that? I can blame myself for taking them. And I did... and he kept offering and I kept taking. I don't know how long it was before I started to just take them.

But I did, every time he left the room I would sneak a couple. And he just kept getting worse and worse.

When I found him he was lying in the bathtub. He had… he had cut his, his wrists… All the way up. And I keep saying, well, if I hadn't done this or that or whatever. But, none of that really does me any good now. Does it? Because what it really boils down to is this: I'm still here… and he's gone. Doesn't get much simpler than that does it? I watched him die. I took the pills and watched.

Ya know, Aristotle was right. I cut out half of my soul and drowned it and watched the blood swim up around it. And now all I want to do is cut out the rest. *(Starts putting stuff back in box)* Just close my eyes and let it rush over me. *(Picks up box)* Here's a fact: *(Puts box back on shelf)* even a room that is full – full of all the stuff, the memories you collect over the years can be empty. It's there now, but close your eyes and it's gone. All gone. *(Pulls cord to turn off light)*

THE BOY WITH THE BEAUTIFUL HEART

By James Doyle

The Boy with the Beautiful Heart
By James Doyle

Once there was a boy who wore his heart where everyone could see it. People would pass by and remark how beautiful it was. Some would even ask to touch it and the boy would let them, if only for a second.

But every time it was touched, his heart let out a single drop of blood. The boy let the drop fall into a bucket he carried at his side. These drops were a part of him. He could not let them go.

Each day people would touch his heart.

Each day his heart would bleed.

Each day his heart shrank.

The boy tried to defend his heart. He denied the world. He vowed to keep his heart to himself. But all was in vain. For who can truly defend something so beautiful as a heart?

Each day people would touch his heart.

Each day his heart would bleed.

Each day his heart shrank.

Before long his heart had nothing left to give. It was shriveled and ugly. It was scarred and bruised. It was empty. The boy tore his heart from himself and cast it into the bucket.

One day a stranger came and told the boy, "You are beautiful." The boy looked at the beautiful stranger and pointed to the bucket.

"I see," said the beautiful stranger, "that is beautiful too."

The little boy cried and said, "Then it is yours to have and to hold all the days of your life."

The beautiful stranger took out a bucket. Inside were a heart and all the blood it had shed.

"This is yours," said the beautiful stranger, "to have and to hold all the days of your life."

Mother's Table

by Jason DeMarco

Mother's Table
by Jason DeMarco

my mother always said
  you are what you eat
as a child
  i died and stopped eating

now i know
  you are what you choose to eat
  you are who you choose to eat with
  you are your choices

what is inside is out
what is outside is in

let the banquet begin for all and not some
this life is just a taste of what is to come

THE MAN WHO HEARS VOICES

By R. Banks

The Man Who Hears Voices
by R. Banks

A guy went home from work one night and heard a voice. The voice whispered to him, "Quit your job, sell your house, take your money, and go to Vegas."

So. He quit his job, sold his house, got together all his money, and headed to Vegas. The moment the man got off the plane in Vegas, the voice told him, "Go to Harrah's."

So he hopped into a cab and rushed over to Harrah's. As soon as he set foot in the casino, the voice echoed, "Go to the roulette table." The man did as he was told.

When he arrived at the roulette table, the voice firmly told him, "Put all your money on 17." Nervously, the man cashed in his money for chips and then put them all on 17. The dealer wished the man good luck and spun the roulette wheel.

Around and around the ball caromed. The man anxiously watched the ball as it slowly lost speed, until finally it settled into number... 21.

Then the voice said, "Damn..."

TOP DOWN

By J.M. Dean

Top Down
by J.M. Dean

me? i'm reading you right now. top down. even though you're wearing a hat, i can tell by the way the hair pokes out the sides that you're balding. but that's easy. see i also know you hate it cause it makes you look more like your father. i can tell by the way you raise your eyebrows that you see your hand as clearly as i do. but you couldn't see what's going on in my eyes if you took those shades off and stared me down like medusa. i can see by the shirt you're wearing that your wife does the laundry. i can tell by the way you sit that you've got no real confidence and not much of the fake kind. i can tell by your shoes that you need the money. i can tell by my obvious observation skills that i don't need the money. and i can tell you right now that it doesn't matter either way. because my truth beats your lie.

The You Bet

by Jane-Marie Desidero

The You Bet
by Jane-Marie Desidero

I think the main difference between childhood and adulthood is the consequences. Yes, there are always consequences. But when you're an adult, they're more severe… and you are expected to actually *deal* with these consequences. You can't just walk away.

I'm a gambler. That's how I made my life. Made my money. Met my wife. Paid for the house. Brought home the bacon. Paid for the kids education. It all happened by chance. It all came with risks. Look, nobody's luck lasts forever. But it might last through today… and who knows what will happen tomorrow. Truth is, life's a gamble

Sometimes you win.

Sometimes you loose.

I say bet big.
You may not get another shot.
Go for the win. But remember:

Always
Always
Always

be prepared to lose

In Line

by Sam Munson

In Line
by Sam Munson

I wake up like I never went to bed. This day begins like every other has... like every other will. My dead eyes rise with the sun and the great transportation has begun. Stand in line for life. I find my box and die again. Resting here in my coffee fueled coffin, I am one with the flock. I work. I buy. I vote I die. I meet expectations and wander mindless in silence so loud you can't hear a scream. I am a part of the machine. I am the heart of darkness. I am the zombie apocalypse.

I am a Vampire

By Jedediah Door

I am a Vampire
By Jedediah Door

I am a vampire
Because I dig drills deep into the ocean floor
and suck the life-blood of the earth from its core...

I am a vampire
Because when I see animals and wildlife slick with the blood I have drained
I think about decreased profit margins...

I am vampire
Because I fill my S.U.V. and don't care

I am a vampire
Because I take her money when I don't need it

I am vampire
Because I take his love when he doesn't want to give it

I am vampire
Because it's all about me

I am a vampire
Because when I hit her and see the hopeless
betrayal in her eyes it feeds my next punch

I am a vampire
Because I say yes when she says no

I am a vampire
Because I don't stay for breakfast

I am a vampire
Because I am alive
        ironic?
maybe
but everyone here knows what it means
to hurt someone
to take something that you can't give back
and if you don't you will
        it's one of those things that comes with being human
isn't it funny? To be alive is to be undead.

Bats

By Heather Brooke

Bats
By Heather Brooke

I hate bats

I hate bats even though they eat bugs
So there
I hate them because they are basically flying rats
And I hate rats

I hate bats because they screech in your ear and flap their hideous ugly wings
And get caught in your hair and then you scream and then it screams and then
you're both screaming and sucks! 'cause there's a bat in your hair.

Plus bats suck your blood. And nothing sucks worse than some freaky little creature
leaching on your neck like a drunk frat boy.

And that's why I hate bats

Death of a Poet

By Jerrod M. Dykes

Death of a Poet
By Jerrod M. Dykes

it is dark as pitch and cold as fright
       as bended low
over a fragile light, I wait patiently
       and know salvation is at hand

round my arm with excited deft
       I wrap fast the elastic band
And wait while perfect poison cooks:
       my last temptation left.

a passerby in terror looks, yet
       forces still their eyes away
as mine will roll into my head
       my skin turning pale grey –

now draw up the spoon that feeds
       like Christ with fish and bread
and take this liquor of my need
up with private vampire fang

       in this night of tremor hell
penetrate my deadened vein
       as in the distance church bells
rang out a forgotten tune
in key beneath the full white moon

Dracula Vs. Robert Pattenson

By Judith Diamond

Dracula Vs. Robert Pattenson
By Judith Diamond

Robert Pattenson is the reason hoards of teen girls watched the Twilight movies

The only reason

I guess that makes him special

But if Dracula ever met Robert Pattenson on the street

He would stick his fangs into his neck and drain his blood till he looked like a wet noodle…

Who's special now?

Just sayin'…

The Count (a haiku)

By Jessica May Delphi

The Count (a haiku)
By Jessica May Delphi

Five, Five Syllables
Seven, Seven Syllables
Ah! Ah! Ah! Ah! Ah!

THE AUDITION

By Sophia Landry

The Audition
by Sophia Landry

KATE: Thank you… bye now… *(smile flashes off her face)* And that leaves… only one more. Thank God. *(presses button on intercom)* Next! *(Long pause, presses button)* NEXT! *(under breath)* Damn… *(starts walking to door)* are you flippin' serious Jeanne… *(Emily enters)* NEXT! *(Emily jumps back)* You're not Jeanne.

EMILY: No. I'm next.

KATE: I see. Come in.

EMILY: My name is Emily Bush. No relation. Thank God.

KATE: I voted for Bush.

EMILY: Oh… Well, then I'm just Emily.

KATE: No… you're just next.

EMILY: Okay…

KATE: So, what are you going to be doing for me today?

EMILY: First of all, let me just say I'm thrilled to meet –

KATE: Just perform.

EMILY: Okay. *(She takes a breath)*

KATE: Go!

EMILY: *(she starts to perform)* You know… it's a funny story… about Billy and me…

KATE: Stop.

EMILY: What?

KATE: Stop. Stop everything you're doing it's awful. I can't stand another second. So stop.

EMILY: Oh – why?

KATE: Why? Dear God you want to know why?

EMILY: Yes…

KATE: You're too short…your hair's the wrong color, your performance was affected, and frankly, the script was crap. Who names a character Billy anymore? Honestly.

EMILY: (very sad) Oh. *(starts to cry)*

KATE: Oh Jesus. Don't cry. Don't cry. I don't have time for this. *(Emily cries harder)* Listen... *(hugs her)* You're a beautiful girl. You've got that going for you.

EMILY: *(through sobs)* Thank you.

KATE: And you're certainly very charming. At least you seem sweet enough... *(questions herself, mouths "sweet?")*

EMILY: Thank you Ms. Mahoney. I'm thrilled to –

KATE: Yes. You mentioned that... Look, you don't want the part anyway.

EMILY: I'm a starving actress *what the hell* does not want the part mean?!

KATE: Look, look, it says on the sheet "looking for an ugly girl."

EMILY: No. Does it really say that?

KATE: Yes, look.

EMILY: That's awful.

KATE: I know, we shouldn't refer to people like that, we shouldn't but we do and it's just –

EMILY: Not that –

KATE: Then wha –

EMILY: I was auditioning... for the part... of an UGLY GIRL! *(starts sobbing)* Oh God! My *life*! Damn! I'm SO FRICKIN' HUNGRY! *(weeping uncontrollably)*

KATE: Not again... listen – that's it! You probably just haven't eaten. Let me buy you something to eat. Please. Dinner. Come on, it'll be a... fun... little... date. Just you and me.

EMILY: What? No! I can't possibly go to dinner with you!

KATE: Why not?

EMILY: *(still sobbing)* You *voted* for *Bush*!

KATE: Oh Emily, please stop crying! I voted for Bush but I admit I regret it!

EMILY: *(slowly recovers)* Oh...

KATE: Really? That's what changed your mind...

EMILY: No... No, of course not. It helped but no. It's –You remembered my name.

KATE: Oh – Well I –

EMILY: Dinner then? Your treat if I remember correctly.

KATE: Well… Hell… *(smiles)* Yah, why not… *(on intercom)* Jeanne? Call Benny's and have them save me the next table for two. *(gets the door)* After you… *(as they leave)* that was pretty intense…

OFFICE THE MORNING AFTER

KATE: *(on intercom)* Yes, Jeanne? *(listens)* Put him through. *(picks up phone)* Hi there, so you've had some time to think so… whadaya think? Yah? Fantastic. I think she'll be perfect for the part. Okay… Okay… Okay… Okay… Goodbye… I – Okay. Goodbye. *(on intercom)* Jeanne? Did Emily Bush leave a mailing address with you? She was my last appointment yesterday. Excellent. Send her some flowers and let her know she got the part. *(Emily appears)* It's none of your business how dinner was. But it was very… it was very nice…

DINNER

KATE: So, feel better now that you've had something to eat?

EMILY: Yes, thank you. I've never eaten at someplace this nice.

KATE: It's alright…

EMILY: I like the music.

KATE: Then let's dance. Come on, don't look at me like that, it'll be fun! *(They start to dance).*

EMILY: So, you have to tell me… why did you vote for him?

KATE: Still caught on politics, huh? Well, I suppose it's unusual to see a lesbian vote republican.

EMILY: *(she reacts)* Well, I –

KATE: My mother talked me into it.

EMILY: Fair enough.

KATE: *(Dips her)* How about another glass of wine?

EMILY: Another? *(She comes up, Stop dancing)* Oh no, I really shouldn't. I'm a terrible lightweight.

KATE: Come on… I need another and you have to join me. My treat, remember? Or…

EMILY: Or?

KATE: Or maybe…

EMILY: Maybe we could have that glass of wine back at your place?

KATE: Took the words right out of my mouth.

OFFICE THE AFTERNOON AFTER

KATE: *(telecom noise, pushes button on telecom)* Yes, Jeanne? *(listens)* Of course… send her in. Hello Emily.

EMILY: Hello. I, uh…I got your flowers.

KATE: Yes! Congrats on the part!

EMILY: I thought you said they were looking for an ugly girl.

KATE: Oh! I talked to the producer this morning… convinced him to change it to a good looking lesbian girl. In this business they're basically interchangeable except lesbians are kind of sexy. And he's a man, so that's how I sold it to him.

EMILY: Oh.

KATE: Besides, I figure you're no Meryl Streep but we both know you can play a lesbian girl.

EMILY: Ms. Mahoney, stop. Please stop.

KATE: What? You think you *are* Meryl Streep? Because, that's a pretty deep psychological issue that I'm not sure I'm prepared to deal with.

EMILY: Ms. Mahoney…

KATE: Please call me Kate. Especially after last night, and I'd love to see you again…

EMILY: Ms. Mahoney… STOP!

KATE: What?

EMILY: I am not a lesbian!

KATE: Oh. Well… I… I just assumed… that last night…

EMILY: Last night… last night I was – last night I had a couple drinks.

KATE: Well we both…

EMILY: Yes, well, like I said I'm a terrible lightweight. Practically under the table after my first drink! But who am I to say no, especially to you and... I have to say I... I feel a little taken advantage of.

KATE: Excuse me...?!

EMILY: I don't mean to point fingers but if it wasn't harassment then last night was ra –

KATE: Last night?! But I thought... I –

EMILY: Look, I did what I did and I said what I said because you're who you are and I am who I am and I'm a people pleaser! It's my nature. It's why I want to be an actor. Actors make people happy. They make me happy anyway. I know that sounds juvenile. But that doesn't make it a bad reason... and you... you do not make people happy. You did not make me happy... not yesterday in this office, not last night... Only this morning, when I got your flowers – I'll take the part Ms. Mahoney. But I won't take you.

KATE: Yes. Well... I'm sorry. I –

EMILY: Please don't. Goodbye.

KATE: Please wait. Of course you can still have the part. I've talked to the producer once today and I'd rather not again... ever. Besides, between last night and just now that's the best audition I've ever seen.

EMILY: Like I said, I'll take the part. Goodbye Ms. – Goodbye.

KATE: *(sits back in her desk, presses intercom)* Jeanne? No, no don't send in the next one. Cancel all of my appointments this afternoon. I – I'm going to need some time.

Rough Draft

by Jordan Douglas

Rough Draft
by Jordan Douglas

(John Brown 1 sings "His Truth is Marching On". John Brown 1 is facing back, John Brown 2 front with arms hung through the bars, They are in a prison)

Guard: Hey! Hey you! Wakeup!

John Brown 2: *(Waking up)* When people are left alone *(grabs bars)* for a long time, left with only their flesh and memories... the world starts to change. You start to know things you never thought you'd know, make realizations you'd never thought you'd realize... like how much you hate being alone. *(smiles)* But it's not so bad. See I've got someone keeping me company... and we've been together a long time... *(Has slowly moved back into sleep position, they are now in a classroom)*

John Brown 1: Hey! Hey you! Wakeup! The teacher's taking attendance.

John Brown 2: Huh?

Teacher: Tony Adamson

Tony: Here!

Teacher: Cassandra Bachman

Ashley: Present!

Teacher: John Brown...

Both: Here! *(pause)* What? Who are you? Who am I? Who are you? That's what I said!

Teacher: Children! Shut up now. It seems I forgot to introduce our new student. John and everyone else, meet our second John Brown. He and his family just moved here from Washington DC. *(Dry)* Isn't that exciting? Everyone say 'Hi John.'

John Brown 2: Hi John...

Teacher: Okay... now that all that's done... Take a seat. *(looks)* You! Now! Okay.

John Brown 2: Name stealer.

John Brown 1: I didn't steal your name. My Dad gave it to me.

John Brown 2: Yah... *(Threat)* Well I'll see you at recess. *(Goes behind, comes back out, points to eyes, then to John Brown 1, then a slow burn exit)*

INTRO

John Brown 2: You stole my name!

John Brown 1: Did not.

John Brown 2: Did so.

John Brown 1: Did not.

John Brown 2: Did so.

John Brown 1: Did not.

John Brown 2: Did so.

John Brown 1: Did not.

John Brown 2: Did not.

John Brown 1: Did so.

John Brown 2: Ha!

John Brown 1: Hey! That doesn't count! You tricked me. Well… I… my dad could beat up your dad! He's in the Army.

John Brown 2: No he could not! My dad's in the Navy!

John Brown 1: Liar.

John Brown 2: You liar. For your information he's fighting in 'the war over there' right now. He's fighting to keep us safe and I haven't seen him since he left and my mom cries all the time which makes me cry too sometimes so why don't you shut up!

John Brown 1: Hey… I'm sorry. Don't cry. My dad is away too.

John Brown 2: Really?

John Brown 1: Yah. He left in June. That's only a couple months… but he missed my birthday. I cried too.

John Brown 2: Wow. I guess we have everything in common.

(They stare at each other for a moment. John Brown 1 picks up John Brown 2's hand and they both hold their hands outstretched).

John Brown 1: *(half jokingly)* Almost.

John Brown 2: And from that moment on we were inseparable. Almost. People grow up and apart often at the same time. And as they grow up most young boys have a strange way of becoming their fathers. But not John. I didn't know it, but he had chosen a new father.
(They whistle "His truth is marching on" as they transition)

John Brown 2: I have news! Cassie Bachman is single!

John Brown 1: Oh.

John Brown 2: Well say *something!* She. is. hot. Hell, we've both had a crush on her since… Just ask her out. I would myself, but *you'll* be around here long enough to get past first base. The only base I'll be on is a military base. Basic training starts in two weeks and I want to do this right. No distractions.

John Brown 1: I would, really, I… I just don't think I'm in a state of mind for women right now.

John Brown 2: What? Why? It's not me going away is it? When you think about it, I won't even be gone that long. *(beat)* You're not *(whistles, does a gesture, means gay)* are you?

John Brown 1: No!

John Brown 2: Well, don't get offended. I didn't think so. I was just asking. Not that it would matter to me if you were…

John Brown 1: John, I think I want to be a man of God.

John Brown 2: You think?

John Brown 1: I know. I know I want to be a man of God. You know, like a minister.

John Brown 2: Oh. And they don't like women?

John Brown 1: Yes! Yes… of course they do. Look, I need to keep my head clear. I've got a lot to think about. Besides, if I do this, I want to do it right. Just like you. No distractions.

John Brown 2: Alright. So… like a minister, huh?

John Brown 1: Yah… like a minister.

John Brown 2: Well, Alright.
(They both 'sing' his truth is marching on, no lyrics, staccato, militaristically transition, swap sides, then John Brown 1 behind)

Drill Sgt: Ten-hut! *(head over shoulder)* Alright, listen up you worthless, scumbag, pieces of less than nothing garbage! *(coming out, circles John Brown 2)* I am your drill sergeant and starting now each and every one of you little ballerinas belong to me! *(Head to the left)* Stand up straight you namby pamby prancing sissy-boys. *(Around to back over next lines, over John Brown 2's shoulder.)* You all make me sick you foul little fairies! You momma's boy maggots! It is my job to turn you useless scraps of filth into machines of death. Machines of American warfare! Do you understand me?!

John Brown 2: Sir, yes sir!

Drill Sgt: I can't here you!

John Brown 2: Sir, yes sir!

Drill Sgt: Okay boys. *(laugh)* Welcome to hell. *(goes behind)*

(John Brown 1 counts off and controls John Brown 2's movements as he moves robotically left, then to the ground for four push ups, then up, forward, into a salute, then into holding a gun, then firing it, then holding it, end with head nod.)

John Brown 1: And… One, Two, Three, Four, Five, Six, Seven, Eight! And… One, Two, Three, Four, Five, Six, Seven, Eight! And One, Two, Three, Four, Five, Six, Seven, Eight! And One… And Two… And Three… And Four… Five, Six, Seven, and Eight!

Choir Leader: Open your worship books to page 247.

(John Brown 1 clears throat, sings "His Truth is Marching On" while John Brown 2 is at war in the background, we see him fire a weapon several times around John Brown 1 at members of the audience, we end by John Brown 2 coming from behind, holding a weapon at close range to an audience member and firing, as he recoils they transition, John Brown 2 goes around back of John Brown 1 as he finishes song, spins around other side to front, he is in prison).

John Brown 2: We liked to think of ourselves as brothers, cut from the same cloth. But choir robes and fatigues are not the same cloth. And after awhile what you wear and what you do becomes who you are. Well, if the war was who I was, I don't know myself anymore. The only news I ever hear in here is from… the news. But I might as well watch cartoons.

Reporter B: Here at the National News Network we know 'the war over there' is always on American hearts and minds... which is why we take time to keep you updated.

Reporter A: As most of you already know, 'the war over there' is against 'them.'

Reporter B: They are mostly scary and fearful, but some are terrifying.

Reporter A: They are a threat to our American way of life.

Reporter B: This is why our military launched Operation Institute Liberty

Reporter A: Or O.I.L. for short.

Reporter B: Now we're protecting American values, by sharing American values.

Reporter A: And sharing has *always* been good...

Reporter B: Still confused?

Reporter A: Let's go to the map.

Reporter B: Just where in the world are our troops?

Reporter A: We're here.

Reporter B: Here.

Reporter A: Here.

Reporter B: Here.

Reporter A: Here.

Reporter B: Here.

Reporter A: Over here.

Reporter B: And here.

Reporter A: This whole region up here.

Reporter B: And, ah, yes. This small village right on the border.

Reporter A: While all this may seem confusing...

Reporter B: Just remember to stay strong.

Reporter A: 'The war over there' could last for –

John Brown 1: Ever?

Reporter A: 'The war over there' could last for years.

Reporter B: And years.

Reporter A: And years.

John Brown 1: Is it ever going to end? Is anyone ever going to win this fight? Are they coming back? Yes – but in body bags or with wild eyes. Something isn't right.

Reporter A: But our top story tonight: Controversial young minister John Brown once again finds himself at the center of a political firestorm this week.

John Brown 1: Ladies and Gentlemen: Once I was blind, but now I see. My eyes were opened for the first time when I watched a good man, and my best friend walk away from me and into 'the war over there'.

Reporter A: Speaking from his pulpit at the New Freedom Church, Brown delivered his latest speech; a scathing condemnation of 'the war over there'.

John Brown 1: I realized in that moment that I may never see him again, and that he was not alone.

Reporter A: The speech brought about massive, albeit peaceful protest from his supporters...

John Brown 1: I started to ask myself important questions. Questions like, Why? For what purpose? For whose greater good? For God or man?

Reporter A: ...and brought threats of retaliation from the countless American supporters of 'the war over there'.

John Brown 1: But tonight, I have no questions, no words of my own. Tonight, my best friend has returned from 'the war over there.' So, racked by silence, I recall the words of Dr. King, "'A time comes when silence is betrayal.' That time has come for us."

John Brown 2: I am an American soldier. I serve the people of the United States.

John Brown 1: "I knew that I could never again raise my voice against the violence of the oppressed in the ghettos without having first spoken clearly to the greatest purveyor of violence in the world today -- my own government."

John Brown 2: I am an expert and a professional. I stand ready to deploy, engage, and destroy the enemies of the United States of America in close combat. I am a guardian of freedom and the American way of life.

John Brown 1: "A nation that continues year after to spend more money on military defense than programs of social uplift is approaching spiritual death."

John Brown 2: I am an American Soldier.

John Brown 1: But tonight, we can find hope in one more soldier home safe.

John Brown 2: and I am home.

John Brown 1: Welcome home John.

John Brown 2: What was all *that* John?!

John Brown 1: Don't be so upset. You're back! That's something to celebrate. That speech wasn't meant to get you all riled up. You've been riled up enough. Here, have another drink.

John Brown 2: There's just one problem, John, I'm going back...

John Brown 1: Back?

John Brown 2: Back for another tour... 'over there'.

John Brown 1: What?! Why? When did they tell you?

John Brown 2: They didn't tell me. I volunteered. Look, I happen to believe in what we're fighting for 'over there'.

John Brown 1: Do you? Tell me, what is that exactly?

John Brown 2: To protect the American way of life, our American values, our –

John Brown 1: John, these people don't understand American values. They understand that more of them are dying everyday and we're the ones who are doing it. That's all.

John Brown 2: What do you know? You haven't seen what I've seen! Been where I've been! Where do you get the right to challenge everything I believe in, everything all of these people believe in? At least I'm trying to do what's right.

John Brown 1: What's right? If that's what's right, then you need to learn to do what's wrong. Just stand up, be a man, and say no.

John Brown 2: Are you saying I'm not a man? To hell with you, you're not my father!

John Brown 1: No. But I am a man. Because I have the courage to stand up and make a real difference. I am a man of the word and of my word and I never had to say 'sir, yes, sir'...

John Brown 2: Shut up...

John Brown 1: Or stand in line...

John Brown 2: Shut up...

John Brown 1: Or pay tribute to some false god...

John Brown 2: Shut up...

John Brown 1: Or kill a man to prove it!

John Brown 2: *(pulling out a gun)* Man, I told you to shut up! Say one more word and I'll kill you! I swear I will! You have no idea what it means to be a man! You stand up there talking about things you don't even understand! Things no one will ever understand! This war isn't about you or me, it's bigger than us! One death means nothing in the face of thousands and thousands...

John Brown 1: I don't know who you are anymore. I don't even know your name.

John Brown 2: My name is Sgt. John Brown. And I am a man of my word...
(He shoots, recoil of gun moves them into transition, John Brown 2 in prison, John Brown 1 is humming "His Truth is Marching On" and eventually starts singing)

John Brown 2: When people are left alone for a long time, the world starts to change. My world will never be the same thanks to John. I may see the world through the bars of a cage, but I am not alone. And I may spend the rest of my life in darkness, but I know his light is shining down on me, guiding me, making me a better man.

The Lord of the Flies

By Scott Gunderson

Based on the book by William Golding

The Lord of the Flies
By Scott Gunderson, based on the book by William Golding

(Both turn to face back, heartbeat)

Ralph: Where are we? *(heartbeat)*

Jack: We're on an island. *(heartbeat)* At least I think it's an island. *(heartbeat)*

Ralph: Who knows we're here? *(heartbeat)*

Jack: Our plane went down in flames. *(heartbeat)* Nobody knows we're here. *(heartbeat).*

Narrator: Welcome to the island.

Narrator: Here, our lost boys wait alone in the –

Ralph: Dark. It's so dark I can't see a thing!

Narrator: Soon the darkness was full of claws, full of awful unknown and menace.

Ralph: I… *(heartbeat)* I'm scared. *(heartbeat as Ralph starts to sing, Jack begins to speak)*

Jack: Of course we're all scared sometimes! But fear… Fear can't hurt you…

Narrator: Jack was older than the other boys on the island. His face was without silliness and turning, or ready to turn, to anger…

Jack: Fear can't hurt you any more than a dream.

Ralph: Things are breaking up. I don't understand why.

Narrator: Ralph was intelligent and reasonable. Only a child himself, he was a leader among men.

Ralph: We began well; we were happy. But at night, people are getting scared.

Jack: I'm not talking about the fear.

Both: I'm talking about the beast.

Simon: Stop! There is no beast!

Narrator: Simon, was perhaps the most wise and patient of the boys…

Simon: We should learn to live in peace until we're rescued.

Narrator: Or perhaps he was naïve...

Simon: We have to have <u>faith</u> that we'll be <u>saved</u>...

Jack: We aren't getting saved. Look at you... you're all terrified. Well, be scared because you're like that—but don't be scared of a beast! Am I a hunter or am I not?! *(Simon goes behind, sings, then Jack speaks)* We're gonna have fun on this island. *(R heartbeat)* Understand? *(heartbeat finishes)*

INTRO

(music, heartbeat)

Ralph: If we're scared here it seems to me we ought to have a chief to decide things.

Jack: Yeah. And I ought to be chief.

Narrator: True. The most obvious leader was Jack. But there was a stillness about Ralph that marked him out. So the boys elected Ralph to be their chief.

Ralph: First thing: we've got to make rules... and obey them. After all, we're not savages.

Jack: Talk, talk, talk. All you do is talk. We don't want rules! We wanna have fun on this island!

Ralph: No, Jack. Our plane went down in flames and nobody knows where we are. We may be here a long time. We have to do this right. We have to build a fire, keep the peace, and take care of the little ones. Sam and Eric, you take watch tonight.

Narrator: So... Two of the boys, Sam and Eric, kept watch into the night.

Eric: What day is it, Sam?

Sam: I don't know, Eric.

Eric: How long have we been here?

Sam: *I don't know, Eric. Ugh.*

Eric: Do you think they know our plane crashed?

Sam: SHUT UP. Aren't you having fun on this island?

Eric: Yes...

Sam: Don't you like having no one to tell you what to do?

Eric: *Yes...*

Sam: And having no girls around?!

Eric: YES!

Sam: Then shut up. Let's just have some fun on this island.

Narrator: Meanwhile, deep in the jungle, Jack began to hunt the beast...

Jack: Hey, who's that sitting there?

Simon: Me. Simon. What are you scared of, Jack?

Jack: What are *you* mucking about in the dark for?

Simon: I wanted to go to a place—a place I know. A place in the jungle. To talk to God.

Jack: Well, you better get back. You understand? There's enough silly talk about the beast without the little ones seeing you creeping around—

Simon: What are you scared of, Jack?

Jack: Nothing. *(Jack goes to sharpen knife)*

Narrator: Roger, a boy both complicated and simple, joined Jack on his hunt.

Jack: Roger. Come here. *(Jack cuts open his hand)*

Roger: What's this for Jack? *(Jack paints Roger's face)*

Jack: In the forest. When you're hunting. When you're on your own. Sometimes you catch yourself feeling as if you're not hunting, but being hunted, as if something's behind you all the time in the jungle. So this is for camouflage. Like in war. Now put some on me.

Roger: You don't look half bad.

Jack: This is fun! *(he holds up his spear like a sword)* Hah!

Roger: *(mimics him)* Hah!

Both: (sword fight) Hah, Hah, Hah!

Jack: This is fun!

Roger: Yeah.

Both: We're gonna have fun on this island! Understand? We're gonna have fun on this island, Understand? We're gonna have fun on this island, Understand?

Narrator: The hunters and they danced late into the night... as Sam and Eric kept watch...

Eric: Sam – *(heartbeat)*

Sam: What?

Eric: *Sam – (heartbeat)*

Sam: *What?*

Eric: It's here. *(heartbeat)*

Sam: Don't be stupid...

Eric: I wish I was stupid. *(heartbeat)* But I'm not. It is.

Both: *(heartbeat) The beast.*

> *(Sam and Eric become deeply afraid, they scream and run around the room)*

Narrator: And so, Sam and Eric ran back to camp. To find Ralph. To find safety.

Both: Wake up! Wake up!

Ralph: What's the matter? What's the matter?

Sam: I saw the beast!

Eric: There were eyes –

Sam: Teeth –

Eric: Claws—

Sam: We ran as fast as we could—

Eric: We were so scared!

Jack: YES! This'll be a real hunt! Who'll come?

Ralph: Don't be stupid Jack. What about the little ones? What about Simon?

Jack: Forget the little ones Ralph! Let's hunt!

Ralph: Someone's got to look after them.

Jack: That's right! I will. I'll kill the beast! Kill the beast! Spill its blood!

Ralph: Have some sense! We've got to think!

Jack: No! I'm not going to play any longer. The beast is a hunter. Like me. Anyone who wants to hunt can come too. Remember, the beast could come at any time, in any form! It could even be one of you! *(laughs, a little scary)*

Simon: Stop it Jack! You're not the chief! Ralph is...

Jack: Shut up Simon. You don't even believe in the beast!

Simon: Maybe there is a beast. I don't know. What I mean is... maybe it's only us.

Narrator: The forest vibrated with fear.

Narrator: And it filled Jack with violent pleasure.

Jack: There IS a beast! You think Ralph can kill it? NO. I CAN. We'll feast and hunt and have fires and do anything we want. Who's coming with me? We're gonna have fun on this island!

Ralph: Let him go. He's just trying to make trouble on this island. They'll be back.

Narrator: Back at camp, Ralph noticed something missing. Something small, but important...

Ralph: Simon? Simon? Where's Simon?

Narrator: But it was already to late...

Simon: *(from behind)* I wanted to go to a place... a place I know. In the jungle. To talk to God. *(SImon sings)*

Jack: The beast is among us! Kill the beast! Spill its blood! Kill the beast!

Simon: *(Simon is bound)* No!

Jack: Spill it's blood!

Simon: Jack...

Jack: Kill the beast!

Simon: Please...

Jack: You are a silly little boy, just a stupid little boy. You knew, didn't you?

Simon: The boys only listened to you because they were afraid. There's nothing to be afraid of!

Jack: I know. I'm the reason why things are what they are... I am the beast.

Simon: Jack...

Jack: *(He stabs him in the neck)* We're gonna have fun on this island. Understand?
    (heartbeat, music)

www.ingramcontent.com/pod-product-compliance
Lightning Source LLC
Chambersburg PA
CBHW080734020726
47503CB00010B/2907